New stuff always happens in September.
You get some new clothes, go to a new class,
make new friends. New is great. (Especially when
it comes in purple.)

But when you make enemies with the biggest,
meanest kid in your new class, new really stinks.
That's what happened to me when mean Irene
came on the scene. I used every trick in the Willie
and Tina game book to get along with her, and
NOTHING worked. Until I figured out the best
and only thing to do . . .

In nine scary steps, here's what I did.

Willie

RULE BOOK #6

# How to Face Up to the Class Bully

WILLIMENA RULES!

RULE BOOK #6
# How to Face Up to the Class Bully

By Valerie Wilson Wesley
Illustrated by Maryn Roos

JUMP AT THE SUN
HYPERION BOOKS FOR CHILDREN • NEW YORK

Text copyright © 2007 by Valerie Wilson Wesley
Illustrations copyright © 2007 by Maryn Roos

Printed in the United States of America

First Edition

1 3 5 7 9 10 8 6 4 2

Library of Congress Cataloging-in-Publication Data on file.

ISBN 13: 978-07868-5525-4

ISBN 10: 0-7868-5525-8

Visit www.jumpatthesun.com

*For Jahi and Jomo*

# My Rules Step by Step

Willimena's
Rules

## STEP #1:
# Get Ready for
# a Terrible Time

It was September. Summer was gone and wouldn't be back for months. *Nine* months, to be exact. Hundreds of days. Thousands of hours. Millions of minutes. Why was summer so short? How come good things never lasted, and yucky stuff dragged on forever? Life could sure be unfair.

"Shucks!" I said with a sigh. I was sitting on the bus to school. My sister, Tina, sat next to me. Tina doesn't usually sit beside me on the bus, but today was different. It

1

was the first day of the new school year. Doomsday!

"What's wrong, Willie?" Tina asked.

"School! What do you think?"

Tina sighed then, too. "Well, maybe we should look on the bright side. Think about the great things that happen when school starts," she said.

"Like what?"

"Like all the new stuff you get, for one thing," she said. She tugged a purple, then a glass bead at the end of one of my braids. The glass beads are clear, unlike the purple ones. All of the beads were brand-new. The sun shining in through the bus window made the glass ones sparkle like diamonds.

I had other new stuff, too. The purple beads in my hair matched my new purple sweater. My new purple backpack looked fantastic with my new purple socks. I had a new purple pencil case with lots of purple pencils in it. (In case you haven't guessed it, purple is my favorite color.) Our old bus—yellow, not purple—even smelled new, like fruity bubble gum instead of rotten sneakers. Tina was right. There was a bright side to everything.

But when the bus pulled up in front of our school, a creepy feeling crawled up the middle of my back. Suddenly, I didn't want to go in.

"Now what's wrong?" Tina asked.

"I'm kind of scared," I said in a small voice. I didn't want anybody besides Tina to hear me.

"Scared? Scared of what?" Tina said. She spoke too loudly. The kids in the seat in front of us turned around and stared at me. One of them giggled.

"Willie, you're being silly. You're just going to school, for heaven's sake!" Tina whispered this time. Thank goodness!

"But what if I have a terrible time?" I asked.

"Terrible time? What do you mean?" Tina said.

"What if I don't know anybody in my class?"

"You're bound to know somebody. What are the chances that you'll be in a class where you don't know a single kid?" said Tina.

"But Harriet Tubman Elementary is a really big school. Sometimes kids end up in classes where there are a lot of new kids. Remember the time you didn't know anybody in your class on the first day of school?"

A sad look crossed Tina's face, then disappeared as she grinned.

"But I made friends quickly, remember? Just smile and say hello, Willie. You have to be a friend to make a friend. Nobody knows anybody on the first day of school. You'll make new friends. You always do."

"What if the teacher is mean?"

Tina made a funny sucking sound with her teeth. "Remember last year when you were scared that Mrs. Sweetly would be mean?"

I nodded. My old teacher, Mrs. Sweetly, had seemed mean the first day. She hadn't smiled. She had talked in a loud voice, and she had yelled at me when I came in late, even though I had tried to be on time. All the kids in my class were scared of her. But Mrs. Sweetly had turned out to be really kind.

"She ended up being your favorite teacher, didn't she?" Tina said in her grown-up voice. She uses that voice when she wants to remind me that she's older than me. Usually it gets on my nerves. Sometimes, though, it makes me feel better. This was one of those times.

"Maybe you're right," I said.

"I'm *always* right," Tina said proudly. I turned my head slightly and rolled my eyes so she wouldn't see me.

"What's your new teacher's name?" Tina asked.

"Mrs. Friendly," I said.

Tina threw her hands up in the air.

"Willie, how grouchy can a teacher be with a name like Friendly? Don't be such a scaredy-cat. Get it together!"

"Okay," I said in a quiet voice.

*But what if the teacher was friendly and the kids were mean?*

I didn't ask my sister that question. She was busy slipping her backpack on, and I didn't want to hear her advice anyway.

When I got to school, I stopped in front of the picture of Harriet Tubman that hangs in the school hall. Our school is named after her. She was a courageous woman who was born a slave. She escaped from slavery and led many enslaved African Americans to freedom. Harriet Tubman is my personal hero.

"Good luck, Willie!" Tina shouted with a

wave as she walked down the hall. "Mrs. Friendly's class will be the *friendliest* class you've ever been in."

"Thanks, Tina!" I shouted back. I don't think she heard me. She was too busy laughing with old friends and running upstairs to her new room.

My new room was on the first floor. It was a couple of doors down from my old one. When I passed Mrs. Sweetly's class, I glanced in. Mrs. Sweetly was sitting at her desk. When she saw me, she grinned and waved.

"Have a great year, Willie!" she said.

"Thank you, Mrs. Sweetly, I will." I tried to sound cheerful, but I really wished I could be back in her room with my old friends. I had so many good memories. I had a couple of bad ones, too,

Have a great year, Willie!

but I had forgotten most of them a few days after they happened. If only I could be back with my old friends and my old teacher. There would be no surprises then.

When I got to Mrs. Friendly's room, I took a deep breath, let it out slowly, and walked in. Then I stopped dead in my tracks. I knew only two kids in the whole room. Two kids! How unlucky could a girl get?

Mrs. Friendly was standing in front of her desk. "You must be Willimena Thomas! Welcome to my room," she said. She had a kind smile and a warm voice.

Maybe Tina was right. Maybe Mrs. Friendly was just like her name. Trust my big sister to have all the answers.

I quickly glanced around the room. It was bigger than my old room, and the sun shining in through the windows made it seem bright and cheerful. There were pictures of famous people on the walls. I recognized Langston Hughes, Abraham Lincoln, and Sojourner Truth. Banners with the alphabet written in cursive style hung above the blackboard. A tall bookcase was filled with books and surrounded by red and orange pillows.

I'm really going to like it here, I said to myself.

"Willie, you're going to sit in Group Four," Mrs. Friendly said. "Your name is on the top of your desk."

I hung my backpack and coat on a hook in the back of the room and headed for the group of desks to which Mrs. Friendly pointed. I found my name and sat down in my seat. This was a great room. This was going to be a great year. I wondered if everybody was as happy to be there as me.

I glanced at all the kids in my group and grinned. Nobody smiled back. Millie, a girl I knew from last year, was wearing glasses like mine. She looked as if she wanted to smile but was afraid to.

*What was wrong with these kids?* I wondered.

Then I remembered Tina's advice about being a friend to make a friend. I tried another grin. "Hey, everybody, I'm Willie," I said. "It's really great to be in Mrs. Friendly's class. I was in Mrs. Sweetly's class last year. She was really nice. What classes were all of you in?"

It was as if I were talking to myself. Nobody said a word.

*WHAM!* A girl slammed a dictionary down on her desk. Everybody jumped, including me. The girl was the biggest kid in the group. She wore a white blouse and red ribbons in her hair. Maybe red was her favorite color, the way purple was mine. IRENE was written on the name tag on her desk.

"Hey stinky-winky, pee-wee four-eyes. You don't belong in here with the big kids. And how come you got on all that stupid, dupid purple?" she said.

At first, I didn't know the girl was talking to me. When I realized that she was, my mind went blank. No one had ever said such terrible things to me before. Not even Tina, and she was my *sister!* My face felt hot. I stared down at my desk. Suddenly, I wanted to be anywhere in the world except in Mrs. Friendly's class, sitting across from mean Irene.

## STEP #2:
# Keep Your Problems to Yourself

"Well, girls, how did the first day go?" my dad asked that night at dinner.

I stared at my hamburger without saying anything.

"School was g-r-r-r-e-e-a-t!" Tina said with a grin. "I'm going to l-o-v-e, *love* my new class. Two of my best friends from last year are there, and my teacher is *so-o-o* nice! This is going to be my best year ever!"

"How about you, Willie?" my dad asked.

I gulped down my milk in three swallows.

"Willie, are you okay?" my mom asked.

I stuffed some broccoli into my mouth and chewed hard. I'm not crazy about broccoli, but it will keep you chewing forever. My parents looked concerned, and thankfully Tina didn't give them a chance to ask me anything else.

"And guess what else, everybody. All the kids remember my play from last year, and I'm going to write another one for this class!"

"That's great!" my parents said in unison.

"And I'm going to be class monitor for the whole week!" Tina added.

My dad grinned. "I'm proud of you girls. You are so grown up. You really know how to handle yourselves in new situations!"

I nodded, as if that were true, but I

didn't think it was. I was happy for my sister. But mostly I was glad I didn't have to tell them about *my* first day.

It was Tina's turn to help with the dishes, so after I finished dinner I ran upstairs to start my homework. I grabbed my cat, Doofus Doolittle, on the way to my room. Doofus is great to talk to when you have a problem. He listens without giving advice (unlike Tina), and he never tells your secrets. There are *real* advantages to having a cat for a best friend.

I sat on my bed with Doofus on my lap. Just hearing him purr made me feel better. Doofus licked my fingers the way he always does when he wants me to pet him. I rubbed my nose in his fur.

"I had a bad day today, Doofus," I said quietly. Doofus tilted his head as if he

I had a bad day today, Doofus.

understood what I was saying.

"This mean girl named Irene made fun of me for no reason at all!"

Doofus licked the side of my face.

"I don't know what to do about it."

Doofus licked my nose, then jumped off

the bed and scampered out of the room. He does that sometimes. I don't hold it against him.

I dug my new journal out from the bottom of my backpack, opened it to the first page, and wrote the date at the top. Mrs. Friendly told us we didn't have to write in our journals every day, because she was only going to read them once a week. That was different from the way Mrs. Sweetly did things. She read our journals every day. I could always count on her to know just what I was feeling. Thinking about Mrs. Sweetly made me feel sad all over again.

Finally, I wrote:

Today was my first day of school.
Everybody was OK except ONE KID.

I put "one kid" in capital letters. Then I wrote:

Today was Monday. Maybe things will be
better tomorrow.

I remembered what Tina had said earlier that day about trying to look on the bright side of things. So I added:

Maybe Irene will be friendlier. Dad says
that people act mean when they feel
scared. Maybe Irene was scared because
she didn't know anybody either.

Thinking about that made me feel better. I put my journal away and started my homework.

But Monday was only the beginning.

*     *     *

I shouldn't have been surprised that after that first day of school things got worse. I've been through some terrible times and that's how it usually is for me.

Like the day I organized the neighborhood pet show and all the pets started fighting. Or the time I almost ruined Tina's play. And then there was that fishing trip that ended up being trouble with a capital *T*. But NOTHING was as bad as this first week of school. And it was all because of one person.

Irene!

Every time she got a chance, Irene made fun of me. Mostly she teased me about the way I looked. None of the kids in my group stuck up for me. They just stared at their desks as if they didn't hear her. Maybe they were scared she would tease them, too.

Irene picked on me only when Mrs. Friendly was busy with other kids or left the room. She always teased me in a low voice so that only the kids in our group could hear. It was weird hearing such mean words whispered in such a soft voice.

"Hey, kid, can't you see anything without those *ugly* glasses!" she would say when I sat down at my desk in the morning. She would stretch out the word "ugly" so that it sounded even worse than it was. Millie had glasses like mine, but Irene didn't tease her. Maybe it was because Millie was taller than me.

And that was another thing. She always teased me about how "small" I was.

"Hey, itsy-bitsy, ditsy-witsy, little, wittle Willie! Go back to kindergarten where you belong!" She said that at least twice a day.

Maybe I wasn't the biggest kid in the class, but I sure didn't look like I belonged in kindergarten!

Then she'd start in on my favorite color.

"Hey, kid, you must stink! Only smelly people wear stinky colors."

Purple is not a person or thing. How could it smell? But it is my favorite color, so I took *that* very personally.

The *first* bad thing was that she made me feel bad about myself. Every time she opened her mouth, I felt like covering my face with my hands. I'd never felt that way before.

The *second* bad thing was that I couldn't think of anything to say back. I just sat there as if my lips were glued together with paste. I felt really dumb. Probably looked that way, too.

The *third* bad thing was that I was too embarrassed to tell anybody about it. I sure didn't want to add Crybaby and Tattletale to the list of names Irene called me.

But each night I wrote down in my journal the mean things Irene had said.

MEAN IRENE LIST

| | |
|---|---|
| Tuesday | Made fun of my glasses and my lunch. Pretended to throw up when she saw me. |
| Wednesday | Teased me about my name. Said I smelled like turnips. Said that kindergarten junk again. |
| Thursday | All of the above and worse!!! |

"Hey, Willie, is everything okay?" Tina asked me on Friday as we walked home from the bus stop after school. Next to Saturday, Friday is my favorite day. I usually have a big smile on my face on Friday.

"I'm fine, Tina," I said, even though it wasn't the truth.

Tina studied my face carefully, the way she does when she knows I'm lying. "Are you sure, Willie?"

"I said I was okay!" I snapped.

"Suit yourself, grouch-a-rouch-o!" She shrugged her shoulders and skipped down the sidewalk to our house.

Lucky Tina. She could afford to skip. She didn't have a thing to worry about. Not like me. Because tomorrow was Saturday, and then came Sunday, and then came Monday. And Monday meant mean Irene!

## STEP #3:
# Don't Be Yourself

Over the weekend, I did all the stuff I love to do. On Saturday morning, I got up early and helped my dad make pancakes. Later I went to the library with Tina and my mom to pick out new library books. My best friend, Amber, and I played *five* games of checkers, and I won every single one! I played hide-and-seek in the Greenes' backyard until it was too dark to find anyone. The Greenes live across the street. We all laughed and had a lot of fun.

But I was still worried. I knew that I

needed a plan for school, and I needed it quick.

In the back of my mind, I kept trying to think of a way to keep Irene from teasing me. On Sunday night, I finally got an idea. It was so simple I wondered why I hadn't thought of it before. If Irene teased me because of who I was, I'd change the way I looked. That would take away her ammunition and zap her good!

Tina and I share a room, and usually she gets up before me in the morning. But this time I got out of bed first. I didn't want to answer any of her nosy questions. As I went over my plan in my head, I painfully recalled each awful thing Irene had said about me. I'd need to change every single one.

My first move was to grab a bunch of

tissues from the bathroom. I folded them into squares and tucked them into my sneakers. Then I pulled on my thickest socks and the bulky sweater I wear on snow days. It was hard to tell if I looked bigger, but I felt as though I did. Irene sure wouldn't be able to call me small anymore.

I searched through my closet for something new to wear. Purple was *definitely* out. But nearly all my new school clothes were purple, and last year's things that were a different color were too small. I sneaked over to Tina's closet and carefully opened the door. But I wasn't careful enough.

"Stop, right there!" Tina yelled. "What do you think you're doing?"

"Can I borrow something to wear to school today?"

"What's wrong with your stuff?"

"Everything is purple."

"But purple is your favorite color!"

"*Was* my favorite color. I'm sick of it." I tried to sound as though I meant it. "Please, Tina, *please*." I hate to beg Tina, and she knows it. She sat up and studied my face, trying to see if I was lying.

"Willie, what in the world is wrong with you?" she asked after a minute. "You've been so grouchy lately. And now you get up before me, and then stuff toilet paper into your sneakers, and then—"

"You saw me stuffing my shoes?" I asked, horrified. "Anyway, it was tissue, not toilet paper!"

Tina ignored me. "And now you're sick of purple. Exactly what are you up to?" It was her trying-to-be-grown-up voice. But I couldn't let myself get annoyed this morning. I had to do some serious deal-making.

"Tina, if you let me wear something of yours, something that's not purple, I'll give you the . . . the five bucks Grandma gave me last month," I said.

"I thought you were going to put that money in the bank." Tina looked skeptical.

"I changed my mind."

"Forget about the money," Tina said. "If wearing something of mine is that important to you, take whatever you want. Just keep your hands off my turquoise stuff. And wake me up in fifteen minutes," she added as she pulled the cover over her head.

Every now and then, Tina will say something that makes me proud to be her sister. This was one of those moments.

I searched hard to find something of Tina's that fit. Finally, I spotted an old sweater that had fallen on the floor. It was wrinkled and didn't have many buttons, but it was red—bright red—and that was good. Irene always wore red ribbons in her hair. Red was probably her favorite color, so I was sure she wouldn't make fun of it.

I slipped Tina's old sweater over my bulky one and glanced at myself in the mirror. I looked kind of weird, but I didn't look small, and I wasn't wearing purple.

There was one last thing I'd have to do, but that could wait until I got to school.

When I sat down for breakfast, my mom stopped eating and looked at me strangely.

"Aren't you going to be hot in all those clothes?" she asked.

Aren't you going to be hot in all those clothes?

"What clothes?" I drank my orange juice and tried not to look at her.

"That thick top . . . Isn't that one of Tina's old sweaters?"

"I told Willie she could wear it. She's trying out a new look," Tina said as she came into the room. She poured some cereal into her bowl and winked. That wink meant I owed her.

"A *new* look wearing an *old* sweater?" My mom sounded puzzled.

"I really love red, and this was the only red sweater I could find. Please let me wear it," I begged.

"So, Willie is sick of purple!" my dad said, sitting down beside me. "Well, if you've got to have a new look, red is a good choice. It's a big, bold color."

Leave it to my dad to make me feel better. My mom still looked doubtful, but I still kept wearing Tina's sweater. So far, so good.

I felt as big and bold as Tina's red sweater when I got to school and walked toward Mrs. Friendly's classroom. But there was that one last thing I had to do.

I took off my glasses and carefully placed them in my backpack. It was hard to see anything without them, but if I wasn't wearing my glasses, Irene couldn't tease me about them. Squinting was a small price to pay.

Bad luck struck as I headed toward my desk. Some kid had left a chair in the aisle, and I was squinting so hard I tripped over it. The good thing was that I caught myself before I hit the floor. The bad thing was that I bumped smack into Irene.

"Look out, fool!" she said. "Better put on your dumb glasses so you can see something. And where did you get that *uugglleeyy* old sweater? The city dump?"

Then Irene did something she had never done before. She shoved me. She pushed me so hard I fell down, right on top of my backpack.

"Aaargh!" I yelled, before I could stop myself.

Mrs. Friendly looked up and rushed over to us. "What is happening over here?" she demanded in a loud, angry voice. She searched everyone's face for answers. Nobody said anything. Everybody pretended to be reading.

"Willie, tell me what happened!" she said, looking down at me. I hoped she would guess that Irene had pushed me. But she didn't.

I glanced at Irene. She was staring at me so hard I could almost feel heat. I knew that if I told Mrs. Friendly the truth, things might get worse.

"Nothing. I . . . I . . . just tripped."

I picked up my backpack and looked inside to make sure my glasses were okay. But I didn't put them on. I didn't want to see anybody in my group. Especially Irene.

"Are you sure you're okay?" Mrs. Friendly asked.

"I'm sure," I said in a small voice. Mrs. Friendly went back to her desk. She told us to take out our workbooks.

I hung up my backpack, then came back to my seat and opened my book. I tried to do what Mrs. Friendly said, but the only thing I could think about was mean Irene— and how my plan hadn't worked and nothing had changed.

## STEP #4:
# Forget Your Sister's Good Advice

It was bedtime. My mom tucked us into bed and closed the door behind her. I listened to her footsteps as she walked downstairs. Tina was listening, too. I could tell, because the moment I heard Mom's foot touch the bottom step, Tina sat up in her bed.

Our room was dark, but I could feel Tina's gaze cutting through the darkness. I hoped Tina would think I was asleep.

No such luck.

"You owe me for this morning," she

whispered. "I know you're awake. I can hear you breathing."

"People breathe, even when they're asleep," I said.

Tina laughed. "Now I *definitely* know you're awake!" She climbed out of her bed and settled herself on the edge of mine. Whenever she does that, I know she means business.

"What do you mean, I owe you?" I said.

"You owe me for covering for you."

"Okay, I'll 'pay' you later," I said, hoping she'd leave me alone.

"That's not all. You owe me an explanation."

"About what?"

"About the weird stuff you've been doing all day. About why you said you were sick when you weren't. That was a bald-faced lie, Willie. You are a better person than that."

Tina was right. It's a terrible thing to lie, especially to your mom. The words had just kind of tumbled out of my mouth before I could stop them. After what had happened that day at school, lying seemed like all I could do.

After dinner, I'd told my mom I had a sore throat. I'd followed that by telling her I had a "stomachache" before I took my bath, then finished the story off with a "headache" when Mom kissed me good night. I'd stared at the light above her head each time I lied. I hadn't wanted to look my mom in the eye.

"We'll see how you feel tomorrow, Willie. You may need to stay home from school," my mom had said. She had really been

worried, which made me feel awful. I felt
bad about lying. But I felt worse about
facing mean Irene in the morning.

"Well, Willie, I'm waiting," said Tina.
Then my sister did something she doesn't
do often. She lay down next to me and took
my hand in the dark and held it. She knew

that that would make me feel better, and it did. "Whatever it is, I promise I won't tell Mom and Dad. You can trust me."

I took a deep breath and spilled my story.

"There's a mean girl in my class who always makes fun of me. She teases me about being the smallest kid and calls me four-eyes because I wear glasses. She says I smell because purple is my favorite color, and today she pushed me so hard I fell down on my backpack and almost broke my glasses." There: it was out, and I felt better.

"Broke your glasses?"

"I had hidden them in my backpack."

"Willie, that wasn't very smart. Glasses cost a lot of money."

"Is that all you care about, my dumb glasses?" My feelings were really hurt.

"Of course not, silly. I care about you. You're my sister!"

After she said that, Tina didn't say anything for a while. When she spoke, I could tell she felt almost as bad about Irene as I did. "So that was why you stuffed your shoes with toilet paper and borrowed my old red sweater. You wanted to look like a different person."

"It was tissues," I said, then nodded.

"What's this kid's name?" Tina went from sad to mad in one minute.

"Irene."

"Irene what?"

"I don't know. I just call her mean Irene. What should I do, Tina? I don't want to go to school anymore."

It didn't take Tina long to come up with an answer. "Irene is a bully, and the best way to handle bullies is to tell a grown-up. You've got to tell Mom and Dad," she said.

"No! I don't want them to know, and you promised you wouldn't tell them, either. You promised!"

"But why not?"

"Because—because it makes me feel like

I can't stand up for myself. And Dad said he was proud because we were grown up and knew how to handle ourselves in new situations. I don't want him to be disappointed in me. And anyway, what can Mom and Dad do about it? If they come to school and tell Mrs. Friendly, things will get really bad. All the kids in my class will think I'm a wimp and a tattletale. I'll never make new friends. Don't you have any other ideas?"

I can always count on Tina to come up with something. Sometimes her ideas stink, but every now and then they're really good. I was hoping for a good one.

"If you won't tell a grown-up, you'll have to handle it yourself," she said.

"How?" I cried.

Even though I couldn't see her, I knew

Tina's eyes had narrowed. She does that when she's ready for a fight.

"Here's what you do. When Irene calls you a name, you call her a worse one. You can't help the fact that you wear glasses. When she makes fun of your glasses, find something about her that she can't change. Something that will hurt her feelings. Make fun of that! And when she shoves you, shove her twice as hard. Push her to the floor! Got it?"

"But she's bigger than me," I said.

"Remember that fight we had a couple of months ago?"

Did I ever. It had started off with a *little* push and a *little* shove. Then the pushes and shoves had gotten bigger. Before we knew it, we were in a TERRIBLE fight. We had both ended up being punished. Afterward,

I had felt really bad about it. I didn't like it when Tina and I fought. It always made me sad.

"Fight like you did that day. Put everything you've got into it. Stomp her!"

"Stomp her?" That sure didn't sound like something I wanted to do, not even to mean Irene.

"It's up to you to uphold the family name. Make me proud of you, little sister. Make me proud!"

Tina had gotten carried away with the sound of her own voice. I knew that when she threw in the "little sister" bit. But it sounded like a good idea.

"I'll do my best," I said.

Who knew? Tina's "good advice" just might work. Whatever happened, I had to take a stand.

## STEP #5:
# Follow Your Sister's *Dumb* Advice

When my mom asked me how I felt the next morning, I told her I was fine. I was through lying to my mom. I was through stuffing sneakers with tissues, too. It hadn't done any good anyway. I was going to take Tina's advice and face up to Irene on her own terms. Mean Irene meets wicked Willimena!

But I sure wasn't ready to "stomp her" the way Tina said I should. I really hate to fight. It never makes things better. You can *really* get hurt, too. I've had enough fights with Tina to double-, triple-prove that.

When Tina and I fight, we really don't mean it. We know we'll be friends again, because we're sisters. That wouldn't happen with Irene.

I was scared on the way to Mrs. Friendly's class. I was *really* scared when I didn't see Mrs. Friendly. She must have stepped out of the classroom for some reason. Suddenly, I was expecting the worst, and I got it.

"Hey, Baby Willie, how come you're wearing that *uugglleeyy* purple again?" Irene said, in the quiet voice that always sounded angry. I glanced at the kids in my group. As usual, they were busy looking somewhere else. I unpacked my backpack, then hung it up and slowly walked back to my seat. My heart was beating fast.

"Silly Willie is too dumb to talk," said Irene.

I *did* feel too dumb to talk.

From somewhere, I heard Tina's voice: *Look at her hard. Find something about her she can't change. Something that she might feel bad about. Tease her about that!*

I stared hard at Irene, trying to follow Tina's advice. I finally found what I was looking for.

Irene always wore the same blouse to school. It was white but looked gray. Two of the buttons were missing. It looked too small for her, and it was always wrinkled.

*Tease her about that!* I heard Tina say again.

I opened my mouth, ready to say something mean. But the words wouldn't come out. They just stuck in my throat. A bunch of "what ifs" popped into my head instead: *What if Irene couldn't help the fact that her blouse was old and wrinkled? What if that was all she had to wear to school? What if her mom and dad didn't really care enough about her to get her new clothes? What if she didn't* have *a mom and dad?*

Irene stared back at me, her eyes angry. "Stop looking at my blouse," she said. She stepped closer to me. She was almost standing on my toes. I could feel her breath on my forehead. Then she pushed me hard against my desk. I fell back against my chair and almost knocked it over.

"You gonna take that, Willie?" whispered Joe, the boy who sat next to me. It was the first thing he'd said to me since school had started, and it made me remember Tina's words: *When she shoves you, shove her twice as hard. Push her to the floor!*

I closed my eyes tight. Then I shoved Irene as hard as I could. I put everything I had into it. I tried to knock her to the floor, just like Tina had said.

*Rrrrippp!*

I opened my eyes. Irene was sitting on the floor. The sleeve of her blouse was nearly torn off. She must have caught it on something as she fell. That was when Mrs. Friendly came back into the classroom. She started waving her hands in the air, and ran over to where we were standing.

"What is going on here?" she yelled. She stooped to help Irene get back up.

"Look what Willie did to me! She made me tear my blouse!" Irene cried.

I stared straight ahead. I didn't know

what to say or do. I hadn't meant to make Irene tear her blouse. It had just happened. *Should I apologize?* I wondered. But she had shoved me first!

I glanced at Irene's face, and then I saw something I never would have believed in

a thousand years. A tear rolled down her
cheek. She quickly wiped it away.

"Who is responsible for this?" Mrs.
Friendly demanded.

"Willie shoved me, and I fell down,"
Irene said.

"Irene shoved me first," I said.

Mrs. Friendly looked at me, then at Irene, then back at me.

"I'm going to let Mrs. Morris sort this out!" she said angrily. "You two girls are in big trouble. You can explain your actions to the principal of the school! Fighting is *never* allowed at Harriet Tubman!"

Everybody in the room was quiet. It was as if all the kids had caught their breath at the same time. I felt my face get hot. I stared at the floor as the three of us marched down the hall to see the principal.

It was the longest walk of my life.

## STEP #6:
# Don't Tell the Principal the Whole Story

I'd been to Mrs. Morris's office only twice before. Both times were for good stuff. The first time was when I lost my sweater, and had to look in the lost and found. The second was when I brought her a note from Mrs. Sweetly.

"Mrs. Morris, I'd like a word with you," said Mrs. Friendly when we got to the school principal's office. Mrs. Morris usually has a smile on her face. When she talks, she sounds as if she's going to burst out laughing. But she wasn't smiling this morning, and I couldn't hear any laughter in her voice, either. All I saw was the frown on her face.

Mrs. Friendly pointed to two chairs next to Miss Wells, the office secretary, and Irene and I sat down. Mrs. Friendly and Mrs. Morris went into her private office. Miss Wells glanced at me, then at Irene, and shook her head.

Irene leaned toward me. For a moment, I thought she was going to apologize. Boy, was I ever wrong!

"I'm going to get you for this," she whispered in her soft, mean voice.

"Are these the two troublemakers?" Mrs. Morris asked when she came out of her office with Mrs. Friendly.

*Troublemakers?* How had I sunk so low?

Mrs. Friendly nodded.

"I'll send them back to your class when I'm finished with them," Mrs. Morris said.

*Finished with them!* I felt like crying.

"Irene, I'll speak to you first," Mrs. Morris said. Irene followed Mrs. Morris into her private office. She looked really small as she walked behind the principal. It was weird. I'd been so scared of Irene I'd forgotten she was just a kid, like me.

As I waited my turn, questions raced through my mind: *Why had I followed Tina's dumb advice? Why hadn't I thought of something better to do? Why had things come to this?*

It seemed to take forever for Mrs. Morris to finish talking to Irene. When Irene came out of the office, she stared straight ahead. I could tell she was trying

hard not to look at me. I knew she had blamed me for whatever had happened when she talked to the principal.

"Miss Wells, would you please give Irene a pass?" Mrs. Morris said. Then she turned to me. "Willie, I'll see you now."

My legs were shaking so hard I didn't think I could stand up. Somehow I followed Mrs. Morris into her office. I tried to look at the walls instead of at her. They were decorated with paintings done by kids in the school. I even spotted one that I had done two years ago.

It was of me and Doofus Doolittle, who in the picture was wearing a red ribbon around his neck and a big smile on his face. It made me want to smile, too. Then I remembered why I was there.

"Have a seat, Willie," Mrs. Morris said.

She nodded toward the chair across from her desk. It must have been made for a really big grown-up and not a kid. It took me a while to sit in it right.

Meanwhile, Mrs. Morris sat behind her desk. She cleared her throat. Then she got to the point.

"Irene said you pushed her and tore her blouse. Is that what happened?"

"No!" I practically screamed. "I pushed, her but I didn't tear her blouse. She tore it when she fell."

Mrs. Morris looked at me as if she were trying to read my mind.

"That doesn't sound like you, Willie. What made you push Irene?"

I didn't want to tell her the whole truth, so I told her a little bit of it.

"Somebody told me to."

"Somebody in your class?"

"No," I said quietly.

Mrs. Morris looked puzzled. "Then, who?"

I didn't answer. No way was I going to get Tina in trouble. She had just been trying to help.

"Who in the world would give you such terrible advice?"

I shrugged my shoulders.

"Did Irene do something to you first?"

"She pushed me."

"She says you pushed her first and made her fall. Who is telling the truth?"

I shrugged again. The more I told about mean Irene, the more in trouble I got!

Mrs. Morris didn't say anything for a long time. When she spoke, she sounded sad. "Willie, I'm very disappointed in you, and I'm sure your parents will be, too. I'm going to call them and tell them what happened."

"No! Do you have to tell my parents, Mrs. Morris? Please don't tell them," I begged.

"You know that fighting is not allowed at Harriet Tubman," she said in a stern voice. Then she said the words that really got to me. "The woman for whom this school is named would *not* be proud of you today!"

Miss Wells gave me a pass to return to Mrs. Friendly's room. I took a long time getting back. When I passed the picture of my personal hero, I tried not to look at her.

## STEP #7:
# Do the Right Thing

Mrs. Morris didn't scare mean Irene. When I got back to Mrs. Friendly's class, Irene stuck her tongue out at me. Then she said: "Tomorrow!"

When school was over, I grabbed my backpack and ran to the bus as fast as I could.

I didn't want to talk to anybody. I sat behind the bus driver and stared out the window. I studied each house, tree, and stop sign as if I hadn't seen them a thousand times before. Finally, the bus stopped on our street, and I ran out the door without saying anything.

Tina caught up with me as I headed toward our house. "What is wrong, Willie?" she asked.

"Nothing," I mumbled. She would find out soon enough. Everybody would.

Peanut-butter-and-apple-jelly sandwiches were sitting on the kitchen table when we got inside. Our babysitter, Mrs. Cotton, had made them for us. A pitcher of chocolate milk stood next to the sandwiches.

"Willie, do you want to eat something?" Mrs. Cotton asked as she does every day. I usually say yes, but not today.

"No, thank you," I said. I hung up my coat and ran straight to our room and closed the door. Finally, I was alone. I didn't have to talk to anybody, and

I hoped nobody, not even Tina, would come.

I pulled my journal out of my backpack. Then I wrote:

This has been a bad, bad, bad, bad day! And it's going to get worse.

I got in trouble for pushing Irene even though she pushed me first. Mrs. Morris is disappointed in me. She said my personal hero, Harriet Tubman, would not be proud of me, either. When my parents get home from work, they're going to be mad. I'll probably be on punishment for a year.

And mean Irene said she is going to get me tomorrow!

WHAT AM I GOING TO DO????

I put my journal into my backpack and glanced at the clock. My parents would be home in an hour and a half. I did my homework; it took a long time. I tried to read my library book, but I couldn't concentrate. I tried to take a nap, but I couldn't go to sleep. Even Tina knew to stay away. She didn't come into our room at all. Finally, I heard the sound I'd been dreading.

It was a knock at my door.

"Willie, your mother and I would like to talk to you downstairs. I think you know what it's about," my dad said through the door.

"I'll be down in a few minutes," I said.

"Now!" said my dad. I could tell he was mad. I waited until I heard him go downstairs; then I slowly opened my door. Doofus Doolittle stood outside. I picked him up and hugged him tight.

"I really need a friend now," I whispered

in his ear. He licked my cheek. It made me feel better, but not much better.

When I got downstairs, my parents were sitting on the living-room couch. The chair across from them was empty, as if waiting for me to sit in it. Doofus Doolittle jumped out of my arms and ran out of the room. He was scared, too, it seemed. I watched him scamper around the corner. I was glad Tina wasn't around. I didn't want her to hear all this and see me in such deep trouble.

"We spoke to Mrs. Morris this afternoon. I want you to tell us what happened at school today," my mom said. She didn't sound mad; she just sounded as if she wanted me to tell her why.

I thought of what my dad had said that first day of school—how he was proud of

Tina and me because we had really grown up. I didn't want him to be disappointed in me. But maybe it was time to tell the truth.

"There's a girl in my class named Irene who teases me. She pushes me, too, and she made me fall the other day," I said in a small voice. "She makes fun of me all the time. I really, really hate school now, all because of her!" Even though I had said the words myself, they surprised me. I hadn't really *loved* school all that much before, but mean Irene had actually made me hate it!

My parents looked at each other and back at me. Nobody spoke for a while. Then my dad said, "Irene sounds like a bully."

"That's what Tina said," I told him.

"Tina knew about this?" He sounded surprised.

"I told her not to tell you."

"Did you push Irene because she pushed you first?" my mom asked.

I nodded.

"Willie, a person can never beat a bully by becoming one," my dad said in a serious voice. "Fighting makes you just like the bully. Who told you to bully her back?"

I didn't say anything. Luckily for Tina, my parents didn't push it.

"The important thing is that you've finally done the right thing," Mom said. "You took the first step to make the bullying stop. You told us about it."

"But why does she pick on me?" I asked.

"A bully will pick on anybody who she thinks she can bully," my dad said. "But the bully is the one with the problem, not you."

"But why me?" I asked again.

"There could be lots of reasons. Sometimes bullies pick on people who they think don't have any friends," Mom said.

I thought about it for a moment. I really had tried to make friends. Once, during lunch, I had given Millie one of my cookies, and she had given me a box of raisins. Not the best trade in the world, but it was something. I had let Joe borrow my eraser. He had let me use one of his crayons. I could tell that both he and Millie wanted to be friends with me, but something was stopping them. Maybe they were scared that Irene would start making fun of them, too.

"Sometimes they pick on people who are smaller than them," my dad added. "Bullies aren't smart enough to know that real strength doesn't come from being big, but from being the best person you can be and having the biggest heart."

"Is Irene the reason you have been so unhappy?" Mom asked.

"Yeah. I didn't know what to do," I said.

"We are going to talk to Mrs. Friendly and Mrs. Morris and tell them what you told us," Mom said.

"No! Please don't tell Mrs. Friendly. She might yell at Irene, and the kids in my class will know I'm a tattletale!" That worried me almost as much as facing mean Irene.

"You are not a tattletale, you just did what was right. We'll ask Mrs. Friendly to make sure the other kids don't find out, but it's very important that Mrs. Friendly know what's going on, because Irene probably bullies other kids, too," my dad said.

I thought about how nobody said much in my group. The other kids were probably just as scared of Irene, too.

Tina came into the living room. I wondered if she had heard the conversation. Knowing my nosy sister, she probably had. But it didn't matter. I felt better about things anyway.

"When is dinner?" Tina asked.

"It's ready now," my mom said. Tina and I helped her set the table. I hadn't realized how hungry I was until I sat down to eat.

After dinner, my dad helped me find some information online about bullies. I couldn't believe how much stuff came up when I typed the word "bully" into the search-engine page.

All of the Web sites said that the most important thing to do if you are bullied is to tell a grown-up. Kids weren't supposed to handle that kind of stuff by themselves. The Web sites said what my dad had said, that the bully was the one with the problem, not the kid being bullied. Most of the sites said that bullies are everywhere, and that everybody—even grown-ups—could encounter bullies in life.

After my mom had tucked us into bed later that night and gone downstairs, Tina got up and came over to sit at the foot of my bed.

"Aren't you glad you finally told Mom and Dad about mean Irene?" she asked.

"Were you listening? I didn't see you anywhere."

"You always listen when I get yelled at,"

Tina said. "Plus, I've got to keep my hiding places secret."

There wasn't much I could say to that.

"You should have followed my advice and told them in the first place," she said after a minute. Trust my big sister to remind me when she's right. "So they'll talk to Mrs. Friendly soon, and everything will be okay," she said with a yawn. She got back into her own bed. A few minutes later, she was asleep.

There was still one thing troubling me. It was great to know my parents were on my side. It was great to know they were going to talk to Mrs. Friendly and Mrs. Morris. But I had to face mean Irene first thing in the morning. I would need to stick up for myself. Again. But this time in the right way.

## STEP #8:
# Look Up, Not Down!

Before I left for school the next morning, I wrote in my journal some of the information about bullies that my dad and I had found online. Here is what I wrote:

> HOW TO FACE UP TO A BULLY
> (after you tell a grown-up!)
> 1. Stand tall.
> 2. Take deep breath when bully comes.
> 3. Look bully in eye.
> 4. Say, "DON'T CALL ME NAMES ANYMORE!!!"

5. Make friends with a couple of kids.

6. Smile.

I added "smile" because it feels good to smile—better than being scared. Then I picked my purple sweater up from the floor of my closet and put it on, and added my purple socks, too, just for luck.

"Good morning, Willie, I see you're wearing your favorite color again. You really look nice!" my mom said when I came down for breakfast.

"Thanks, Mom," I said. I sat down and took a big spoonful of oatmeal. I'm not a big fan of oatmeal, but I needed all the strength I could get.

"We'll talk to Mrs. Friendly today after school," my dad told me as Tina and I left to catch the bus.

Tina sat next to me on the bus. She did that sometimes. That was her way of helping me feel brave.

"Do you want me to walk to class with you?" she asked as we walked into the school. "Maybe Irene should know you've got a big sister. She won't dare pick on you then!" She stood up straight and stuck out her chest, trying to make herself look bigger than she was.

I thought about it for a minute. My parents wouldn't talk to Mrs. Friendly until school was over. I was going to see Irene in a few minutes. Maybe Tina could keep Irene from provoking me.

But Tina couldn't stay in Mrs. Friendly's class the whole day. She had her own class to go to. According to one Web site I'd looked at, I might have to face up to another bully sooner or later anyway. Bullies were everywhere, so I might as well get in some practice.

"No, Tina, I'll be okay," I said.

Tina gave me a hug. "Well, if you need me, you know where to find me."

I nodded and smiled, but a knot was forming in my stomach. It was the one that came whenever I got scared. It was then that I happened to glance up at the picture of my personal hero.

Harriet Tubman had confronted terrible people who did terrible things. And some of the "passengers" on her "train to freedom" had been so scared she had had to force them to go with her. She was one of the bravest women who ever lived. That was why I admired her. Facing up to mean Irene was small potatoes compared to

what Harriet Tubman had battled. I owed
it to her to be brave.

"You'll be proud of me, Mrs. Tubman,"
I whispered to her picture.

I stood as tall as I could. I held my
head high. I put a big smile on my face,

walked into Mrs. Friendly's class, and went to my desk to unpack my backpack.

"Hey, everybody," I said, to nobody in particular. I took out my books and hung up my coat. Irene was ready for me when I got to the back part of the room, where my small group always gathered.

"Hey, stinky-winky, four-eyed Willie in your ugly, dugly purple," she said in her low, mean voice.

I took a deep breath. "What did you say?" I asked. I was acting cool, but my heart was beating fast.

Irene looked surprised.

"You heard me, stinky-winky, four-eyed Willie! Go back to kindergarten with the other babies!"

Slowly, I sat down in my chair. I thought about the words I'd written in my journal that morning. I thought about Harriet Tubman. I looked Irene straight in the eye, and I said, "Don't you dare ever call me that again. I'm sick and tired of your teasing me. Got it?"

Irene rocked back in her chair. She looked surprised. Then she came back at me. "You think about this," she said pointing her finger at me. "I'm going to break you in half, just like this pencil!" She took the pencil that was lying on her desk and snapped it in half. Joe, the kid who sat next to me, gasped. I felt my stomach turn over. Then I remembered Harriet Tubman and the meanies she'd faced up to.

I narrowed my eyes the way Tina does when she gets mad, and I said, "Everybody in our class, in the school, in the whole, wide world really, really *hates* a bully. *You* are the biggest, awfulest, bulliest bully anybody in this class has ever seen. *You* think about that, mean Irene!" I said it as if I meant it. And guess what: I did!

I picked up my library book and pretended to read. My hand was shaking, and I was so scared I couldn't see the words. Then something happened that I wouldn't have believed in a million years.

"Go, Willie. Tell her!" whispered Joe.

Millie, the kid across from me who wore glasses like mine, spoke up next. "There's nothing wrong with Willie's glasses, Irene. I love my glasses. Just like Willie does!"

"I like purple, too, just like Willie," said Dana, another kid. "Don't talk about *our* favorite color ever again!"

Suddenly, everybody in my group was standing up for me—standing up to Irene.

Irene looked scared, as if she were going to cry. For a moment, I felt sorry for her. But just for a moment.

"Too much talking over there!" Mrs. Friendly said. "Take out your workbooks, so that we can begin the day."

Everybody got quiet. We opened our workbooks as Mrs. Friendly had told us to. We took out our pencils and started to write—everybody except Irene, that is.

"Somebody, give me a pencil!" she said. She glared at each kid in our group.

"No way! You broke yours in half . . . mean Irene!" said Joe. A couple of kids giggled.

"Will somebody please give me a pencil?" Irene asked. This time Irene was asking, not demanding. But everybody pretended not to hear her.

I thought about what my dad had said about real strength coming from being the best person you could be and having the biggest heart. Maybe it was time for me to be *my* best girl.

"You can have this one," I said. I reached into my pencil case and pulled out a pencil. Just *her* luck it was purple.

"Thank you, Willie," Irene said in a softer tone. But it still took her a long time to say it.

## STEP #9:
# Get Ready for a Great Time

My parents did end up meeting with Mrs. Friendly and Mrs. Morris the way they said they would. After that, things started changing at Harriet Tubman Elementary School.

For one thing, Mrs. Friendly announced that she would read our journals every day unless we wrote: *Private* across the top of the page. She promised she would never tell anyone what we wrote unless we gave her permission.

Some kids didn't like the idea, but I did. It was like having a secret pipeline to a special person. Sometimes, Mrs. Friendly drew a happy face in pink ink at the end of a page to let me know she was listening. Even when she didn't, I knew she was there if I needed her.

We also had a big class discussion about bullying. We read stories about what bullies do and how it feels to be bullied. (Was I ever an expert on that!)

A couple of kids told stories about how bigger kids had picked on them. So I found that I wasn't the only kid in my class who had run into a bully. One kid named James cried when he told us how his big brother bullied him. I guess I'm really lucky to have Tina for a sister. She gets on my nerves, but at least she's not a bully. I told everybody about the stuff on bullying that my dad and I found online. It felt really good to share the facts.

I didn't talk about what had happened between me and Irene. For one thing, everybody in my group knew it. Every time somebody said the word "bully," some kid in my group would turn around and stare at her. For another thing, Irene wasn't bullying me or anybody else anymore. As a matter of fact, she wasn't saying much of anything to anybody.

We also read a story about why kids become bullies. Sometimes they pick on other kids because somebody has bullied them at home. Sometimes it's because they don't feel good about themselves. Bullies usually have trouble making friends, and sometimes they think being a bully will make people respect them. (Boy, are they ever wrong!)

I wondered if bad things had happened to Irene. I remembered how she had cried when her blouse got torn. I wondered if that was the only blouse she had. Maybe she was mad at me because I wore all that new stuff the first week of school. Maybe that made her feel sad, and sad turned into mean. Thinking about that made me feel sorry for her. I wrote about my feelings in my journal to Mrs. Friendly. I also decided I would try to be friendly to Irene.

One morning, our principal, Mrs. Morris, announced over the PA system that she was putting a "Bully Box" in her office. The box was for kids who were being bullied *and* for kids who were bullies. If you were being bullied you could tell the principal who was bullying you. If you were a bully, you could ask for help. The Bully Box would be next to the lost and found so that a kid could slip in a note and pretend she was looking for her mittens.

I was really glad to hear about that. I wondered if Irene would write a note to Mrs. Morris. I really hoped that she would.

I wish I could say that Irene and I became friends, but that kind of thing only happens on TV. Sometimes Irene was kind of nice to me. Other times she was still a little mean. At least I knew that Irene's attitude had nothing to do with me. It was her problem, not mine. All I could do was be kind to her and hope it would pay off someday.

I did make lots of other new friends, though. Once we all started talking to each other, the kids in my group found out we

had a lot in common. Not only did Millie and I have the same glasses, but Harriet Tubman was her personal hero, too. Joe loved granola bars almost as much as I did, and Dana had a cat—though when Doofus and I went over to her house, we quickly noticed that Dana's cat didn't look like Doofus. (It's okay if I'm the only one who can appreciate the one and only Doofus Doolittle's special qualities!)

Mrs. Friendly's class ended up being one of the *friendliest* classes I'd ever been in. So my crazy big sister was right after all.

But there's no way I'm ever going to tell her!

I don't know if mean Irene will ever become nice Irene. But stranger things have happened. Never say never, that's my motto.

I do know that my new friends in my new class are some of the best friends I've ever made. When you're friendly to kids, they're usually friendly back. Most kids. Most of the time.

And that brings me to my dear cousin Teddy and his recent visit on my favorite winter holiday. Teddy had a serious case of the Not-So-Friendly Blues. It was up to me and Tina to try to cure him.

(That's, TRY, in very big letters!)

Willie

What is Cousin Teddy's problem, and why is he wrecking Willimena's favorite holiday? Read all about it in . . .

**WILLIMENA RULES!**

How to Have the Best Kwanzaa Ever (and Christmas, Too!)

Rule Book #7